The Green Guardian

His heart, her haven

P. A. Farrell

Cover photo: Slava Auchynnikau@unsplash.com

The Pocket Companion Series contains:

When Your Mind Won't Stop

After the Loss: Finding Your Way Through Grief

You Are Enough: Rebuilding Your Self-Worth

At the Crossroads: Making Decisions When Nothing Feels Clear

When People Hurt: Navigating Difficult Relationships

When You Feel Stuck: Finding Movement in Hard Times

Books by Patricia A. Farrell, Ph.D.

When You Can't Pour From an Empty Glass: CBT Skills for Exhausted Caregivers

The Little Book on Learning Big Critical Thinking Skills

The Smart Kid's Survival Guide: Making Good Choices in a Confusing World

How to Be Your Own Therapist

P. A. FARRELL

It's Not All in Your Head: Anxiety, Depression, Mood Swings and Multiple Sclerosis

Unfiltered: Beneath the noise of our thoughts lies the true narrative of our minds

Unfiltered Again: A behind-the-scenes look at healthcare, medicine and mental health

A Social Security Disability Psychological Claims Handbook: A simple guide to understanding your SSD claim for psychological impairments and unraveling the maze of decision-making

A Social Security Disability Psychological Claims Guidebook for Children's Benefits

The Disability Accessible US Parks in All 50 States: A Comprehensive Guide

Birding in the US NOW!: A birding guide for individuals with disabilities

Contents

Chapter 1: A New Beginning

Samantha Andrews stood at the base of the shining dark glass office tower, tilting her head back to take it all in. Seventy-two stories of sleek steel and windows that reflected the morning clouds above. Green-Tech Solutions. She had finally gotten through all of the interviews to get this opportunity in the field about which she was so passionate. It was her dream job and she finally got it.

She'd wanted this position for years. Working for a nonprofit had been fulfilling in its own way, but resources were always tight. Every project felt like a fight. But here? GreenTech had the money, the influence, the reach to make real change. And they wanted her to be part of it.

How had she been so fortunate? Of course, she had worked extremely hard in college with knowledgeable scientists and researchers focusing all of her energy on this area. No doubt about it, she had been preparing for this moment for years. It didn't come to her as a fluke but as a well-planned effort to secure a job here. But through it all she wondered why they chose her.

She smoothed her blazer and walked through the revolving doors. The lobby was all marble and chrome, with a water feature running down one wall. A security guard nodded at her from behind his desk, and she smiled back, feeling like she belonged here already. Her name was on the clipboard that he had, and he issued an employee pass after taking her photo, before she could walk through the special security glass panels that opened to the elevator lobby.

The elevator ride to the tenth floor felt both too fast and too slow. It seemed like she had just stepped into the elevator when it was already at her floor. Her stomach fluttered with nerves. First-day jitters. Totally normal. She'd be fine once she got settled. She kept telling herself to calm down and act naturally. How do you act natural when everything you've been hoping for is on the line now?

The doors in the reception area slid open, and a woman about her age was waiting, holding two coffee cups and grinning.

"You must be Samantha," the woman said. "I'm Lisa Miller. Welcome to the team. I brought you coffee because first days are rough, and caffeine helps everything." Really, this was a place that was quite welcoming, and Samantha was relieved.

Samantha laughed and took the cup. "You're my new favorite person." Maybe she could have a coworker and friend in her, and even a confidante.

Lisa was easy to like. She gave Samantha a quick tour of the floor, pointing out the break room, the supply closet, and the restroom. Everything was clean and modern. The offices had glass walls, and Samantha could see people at their desks, working away on computers or talking on phones. The activity level was impressive.

"Here's your office," Lisa said, stopping at a door near the end of the hallway. "It's small, but you've got a window. That's basically gold around here."

Samantha stepped inside. The office was tiny, yeah, but it had a desk, a chair, a computer, and a view of the city. She could see the tops of other buildings and a slice of blue sky. It was perfect. How much better could it get? In fact, from her office she could see through the glass partitions to other people's work areas, and it felt like they were all worker bees in a huge hive. Not a bad thing since hives produced honey.

"I love it," she said.

Lisa grinned. "Good. Let me introduce you to a few people."

The next hour was a whirlwind of names and faces. Everyone seemed friendly enough, though Samantha knew it would take her some time to remember who was who. Then Lisa led her to the corner office, where a man in his early fifties sat behind a large desk. The positioning of the office told her that he was the most important guy on the floor. Now it was time to be on her best behavior and to remember everything that was discussed here.

"Derek Morrison," Lisa whispered as they approached. "The CEO. He likes to meet new hires personally." Not everyone gets to meet the CEO on their first day at work Samantha knew. This was another interesting fact about the company.

Derek looked up and smiled. He had perfect teeth and a suit that probably cost more than Samantha's car. "Samantha! Come in, come in. Lisa, thanks for bringing her by."

Lisa gave Samantha an encouraging nod and left. Samantha sat in one of the leather chairs across from Derek's desk. He sat down on the other side of his desk, relaxed, and began to interview her.

"We're thrilled to have you," Derek said. "Your resume is impressive. Three years with EarthFirst, two years at Green Horizons. You know the nonprofit world, but now you're ready to see what we can do with real resources." So far, so good.

"I'm excited to be here," Samantha said. "GreenTech has an amazing reputation." One compliment deserved another, and she was eager to show she was a happy, enthusiastic new employee.

"We work hard to maintain it," Derek said. "Our commitment to environmental excellence isn't just a slogan. It's who we are. And we need people like you to keep us honest." He laughed, but something about it felt rehearsed.

Why was she getting that odd feeling that her questioning antenna was signaling something to her? Couldn't be. Samantha smiled, anyway. First day. Be positive. Don't overthink things.

"I'm looking forward to diving in," she said.

"That's what I like to hear." Derek stood, signaling that the meeting was over. "If you need anything, my door's always open." With that, she was guided back to her office as he turned away to go back to reviewing a pile of reports.

Back at her desk, Samantha spent the rest of the day settling in. Several report books had been left on the desk for her review. Lisa stopped by a few times to check on her, and by five o'clock, most people were packing up to leave. It didn't seem like people were going to stay late, and she wondered why everyone left promptly at five.

"You coming?" Lisa asked, poking her head in.

"I think I'll stay a bit longer," Samantha said. "Get a head start on some of these files."

Lisa raised an eyebrow. "Overachiever. I like it. Don't stay too late, though. The building gets creepy when it's empty."

Samantha laughed. "I'll be fine."

By six-thirty, the office was quiet. Samantha liked it. No distractions. Just her and her computer and the hum of the air conditioning.

She was reviewing a report on a recent project when she suddenly felt a chill. The temperature in her office seemed to drop ten degrees in seconds. Samantha rubbed her arms and looked around. The windows weren't the kind that could be opened, so there was no way a draft was coming in, and the vent wasn't blowing cold air. In fact, this was a building that was sealed, and air needed to be brought in through the central system.

Weird.

Her computer screen flickered. Once, twice, then steadied. Samantha frowned. Maybe the building had electrical issues. She'd mention it to IT tomorrow.

She went back to reading, but the chill lingered and she knew that tomorrow she'd need to bring a sweater in case it got this cold again. And then she noticed the folder.

It sat on the corner of her desk, a manila folder with her name in neat handwriting. Had that been there before? She couldn't remember. Maybe someone had dropped it off while she was in the restroom.

Samantha opened it. Inside was a report about a GreenTech project from two years ago. Construction of a water treatment facility in a small town outside the city. As she skimmed the pages, some passages jumped out at her. Someone had highlighted them in yellow. Not only had they left an important file, but they had also indicated specific areas to call to her attention. Would have done that?

Waste management protocols abbreviated due to timeline constraints. That was odd. Environmental impact study results pending review.

Local water quality testing postponed until post-construction phase.

Samantha's stomach tightened. These weren't good signs. Abbreviated protocols? Postponed testing? That wasn't how environmental projects were supposed to work.

She flipped through the rest of the report, but there were no notes, no explanations. Just those highlighted passages, like someone wanted her to notice them. Should a new employee have been given this information?

Samantha leaned back in her chair. Maybe it was a test. Maybe Derek or someone on the team wanted to see if she'd catch the problems. That would make sense. They'd hired her to keep them honest, after all.

But why not just hand it to her directly? Why leave it on her desk like this?

She glanced at the clock. Seven-fifteen. Late enough. She'd ask Lisa about it tomorrow.

Samantha packed up her things and headed for the elevator. As she waited, she looked back down the hallway. The office lights were motion-activated, and most of them had already shut off. The entire floor looked dark and empty. Everyone had left.

She shivered, recalling Lisa's comment about the building feeling creepy. No doubt, Lisa was right because this place wasn't welcoming in the darkness.

The elevator dinged, and she stepped inside, grateful to be leaving. First day was over. Tomorrow would be better. More normal.

She had no idea how wrong she was.

Chapter 2: Strange Occurrences

By the end of her first week, Samantha had decided the building had some serious quirks. But she would learn to live with it because after all what building is perfect?

Documents kept showing up on her desk. Reports she hadn't requested. Files she didn't remember opening. Every single one had something concerning in it. Environmental shortcuts. Buried complaints. Impact studies with gaps that made her stomach hurt.

At first, she thought maybe she was being forgetful. New job stress. Too much information coming at her too fast. But by Wednesday, she couldn't deny it anymore. Something weird was going on.

Her computer had a mind of its own. Files would open without her clicking anything. Folders she'd closed would pop back up on her screen. And always, always, they led her to the same kind of information. Problems. Cover-ups. Things that shouldn't have been swept under the rug.

Thursday afternoon, Samantha found Lisa in the break room, pouring coffee.

"Hey," Samantha said. "Can I ask you something?"

"Sure." Lisa handed her a cup. "What's up?"

"Have you ever noticed anything weird about the building? Like, electrical problems or glitches with the computers?"

Lisa laughed. "All the time. The IT system here is ancient. Half the time my computer freezes for no reason. And don't even get me started on the air conditioning. Some days it's a sauna, other days it's Antarctica."

Samantha relaxed a little. So it wasn't just her. "Good to know I'm not going crazy."

"Oh, you'll get used to it." Lisa took a sip of her coffee. "This building has quirks. It's old. Well, not that old, but it's been here a while. Things happen."

"Things?" Samantha raised an eyebrow.

Lisa shrugged. "You know. Office building stuff. Weird noises. Lights flickering. People swear they've heard footsteps when no one else is around." She laughed again, but it sounded a little forced. "Some folks think the place is haunted."

Samantha's smile faded. "Haunted?" This was ridiculous. Everyone in this corporation had a background in science and that meant everything had to make sense and had to be verified with facts. What Lisa was telling her had no factual basis, only people being a bit unnerved.

"Don't look at me like that. I don't believe in ghosts. But someone did die here a few years ago. Guy named Ethan something. I wasn't working here yet, but I've heard about it." Someone had died in this building? And she had never been told about it? But then why would you tell a new hire this?

Samantha's chest tightened. "What happened to him?"

"Accident. He fell down the main stairwell late one night. Working alone or something. It was ruled an accident, but nobody likes to talk about it." Lisa glanced at the clock. "Anyway, don't let it freak you out. Buildings like this always have stories."

Samantha forced herself to nod. "Right. Just stories."

But that night, working late again, the story wouldn't leave her head. Had there been some connection to what that guy was working on and his sudden accident?

She'd found another file on her desk. This one about a factory expansion that had bypassed local zoning laws. Someone had highlighted the section where GreenTech paid off a city councilman to smooth things over.

Samantha stared at the pages, her mind racing. Who was leaving these for her? And why?

The office was quiet. Too quiet. She could hear the hum of the fluorescent lights overhead, the faint buzz of her computer. And then, footsteps.

Slow. Deliberate. Coming down the hallway.

Samantha's heart started to pound. She stood and walked to her office door, peering out. The hallway was empty. The motion-sensor lights were off except for the ones near her office.

"Hello?" she called.

No answer.

She waited, straining to hear. Nothing. Maybe she'd imagined it. Maybe her mind was playing tricks on her after Lisa's ghost story.

Samantha went back to her desk, but she couldn't shake the feeling that she wasn't alone. No it was just the fact that she was here alone and the place was pretty dark that must have been upsetting her. There had to be some sense here.

Her computer screen flickered. Then a folder opened on its own. A file she'd never seen before.

The title made her breath catch: "Ethan Reeves - Final Report." Wasn't that the name of the guy who fell down the stairs?

Samantha's hand trembled as she reached for the mouse. She clicked on the file. It was a personnel document. Ethan Reeves. Senior environmental analyst. Hired six years ago. Died five years ago.

There was a photo attached. A man in his early thirties with brown hair and light brown eyes. He was smiling in the picture, like he'd been caught off guard by the camera.

Samantha stared at the screen. Something about his face felt familiar, though she'd never seen him before. Or had she?

The temperature in the room dropped. That same sudden chill from her first night. Samantha wrapped her arms around herself, goosebumps rising on her skin. Where was that sweater she meant to bring?

"Okay," she said out loud, trying to steady her nerves. "I'm officially creeped out now."

She closed the file, shut down her computer, and grabbed her bag. Time to go home. Get some sleep. Stop letting her imagination run wild.

But as she walked to the elevator, she couldn't shake the feeling that someone was watching her.

And when she glanced back at her office, just before the elevator doors closed, she could have sworn she saw a shadow move across the window.

Chapter 3: First Contact

Samantha told herself she wasn't going to work late anymore. Not until she figured out what was happening. But Friday night found her at her desk anyway, finishing up a report that was due Monday.

The office was quiet again. Most people had left by six. Now it was almost eight, and she was alone on the entire floor. Or at least, she should have been alone.

The cold hit her first. That same sudden, bone-deep chill that made her teeth chatter. Samantha looked up from her computer, her breath fogging in the air. No this wasn't normal. Nobody could see their breath while breathing in an office setting.

Papers on her desk started to move. Not just flutter. They lifted into the air, swirling like a small tornado had formed right there in her office.

"What the—" Samantha pushed her chair back, heart hammering.

And then she saw him.

A man stood across the room, near her door. Translucent. Shimmering. Like he was made of water and light. He wore a button-down shirt and khakis, normal office clothes, but she could see straight through him to the wall behind.

Samantha's scream caught in her throat. She couldn't move. Couldn't breathe. Now her heart was really pounding.

The man held up his hands, like he was trying to calm a scared animal. "Please," he said. His voice sounded distant, like it was coming from underwater. "Please don't be afraid. I need your help."

Samantha finally found her voice. "What are you?" She knew she should have said, "Who are you?"

"My name is Ethan," he said. "Ethan Reeves. I used to work here."

The name hit her like a punch. Ethan Reeves. The man who died. The one Lisa had mentioned.

"You're dead," Samantha whispered.

"Yes." He looked down at his hands, like he was still surprised by his own transparency. "Five years ago. I fell down the stairwell. Or at least, that's what everyone thinks." What everyone thinks?

Samantha's hands gripped the armrests of her chair. This wasn't real. It couldn't be real. She was hallucinating. Maybe she had a gas leak in her apartment. Maybe she'd hit her head and didn't remember. There had to be an explanation.

"I know this is hard to believe," Ethan said. "Trust me, it took me a long time to accept it too. But I've been stuck here since the night I died. Trapped in this building. And you're the first person who's been able to see me."

"Why?" The word came out as a croak. "Why me?"

"I don't know," he said. "But I think it's because you care. About the environment. About doing the right thing. The same things I cared about when I was alive." Caring had opened some kind of portal to this dead person?

Samantha shook her head. "This isn't happening. You're not real."

"I've been leaving you files," Ethan said. "Documents. Evidence. I've been trying to guide you toward the truth."

The truth. Samantha thought about all the reports she'd found. All the highlighted passages. The problems that kept appearing on her screen.

"What truth?" she asked, still not sure if she was losing her mind.

Ethan stepped closer, and Samantha fought the urge to run. "GreenTech isn't what it claims to be. They've been cutting corners for years. Falsifying environmental reports. Paying off officials. I found out about it when I worked here. I tried to expose them, and—" He stopped, his expression darkening. "And I ended up dead."

"They killed you?" Samantha's voice was barely a whisper.

"I don't know," Ethan said. "I honestly don't remember what happened that night. But I know it wasn't an accident. And I know I can't move on until someone finishes what I started."

Samantha stood on shaky legs. "This is insane. You're asking me to—what? Take on the entire company?"

"I'm asking you to do what's right," Ethan said. "The same thing you've been doing your whole career. I've read your file. You've dedicated your life to protecting the environment. This is your chance to make a real difference."

"By listening to a ghost?" Samantha let out a hysterical laugh. "I can't believe I'm even having this conversation." She must be losing her mind she thought.

Ethan's expression softened. "I know I'm asking a lot. And I know you're scared. But please, Samantha. Just think about it. Look at the evidence I've given you. Decide for yourself."

"I need to go," Samantha said, grabbing her bag. "I need to leave. Now."

"Wait—"

But Samantha was already running. Out of her office, down the hallway, into the elevator. She jabbed the button for the lobby, her whole body shaking.

As the doors closed, she caught one last glimpse of Ethan standing in the hallway. He looked sad. Lost. Like he'd been hoping for something and was watching it slip away.

Samantha pressed herself against the back of the elevator, trying to catch her breath. This wasn't real. It couldn't be real.

But deep down, she knew it was.

And that scared her more than anything.

Chapter 4: Acceptance and Investigation

Samantha didn't sleep that night. Sleep was impossible after what she had just experienced.

She lay in bed, staring at the ceiling, replaying the encounter over and over. A ghost. She'd seen a ghost. And not just any ghost—a man who claimed her company was involved in environmental fraud and maybe even murder. And she'd spoken to him.

By the time dawn broke, she'd given up on sleep and grabbed her laptop. If she was going to lose her mind, she might as well do it with facts.

She typed "Ethan Reeves GreenTech" into the search engine.

The first result was his obituary. Ethan Michael Reeves, age 32, died in a tragic accident. He was survived by his parents and a sister. Services were private. In lieu of flowers, donations could be made to the Nature Conservancy.

Samantha scrolled down and found a brief news article. "Local Analyst Dies in Office Accident." The story said Ethan had been working late when he fell down the stairwell. No one witnessed it. Security footage showed him entering the building but not leaving. The death was ruled accidental.

There was a photo attached to the article. The same face she'd seen last night. Brown hair, kind eyes, that smile.

Real. He was real. Or he had been.

Samantha closed her laptop and pressed her hands to her face. This was impossible. Ghosts weren't real. But she'd seen him. Heard him. Felt that bone-deep cold when he appeared.

And if he was real, then maybe everything he'd said was true.

By Monday evening, Samantha found herself back at the office after everyone else had gone home. She told herself she was catching up on work. But really, she was waiting. Would he come again?

The sun had set. Her office was dark except for the glow of her computer screen. Samantha took a deep breath and spoke into the empty room.

"Ethan? Are you here?"

For a moment, nothing. Then the temperature dropped like before.

He appeared near the window, that same translucent shimmer. But this time, Samantha didn't run. She stayed in her chair, hands clenched tight in her lap. She was going to face him and she was going to find out what was going on.

"You came back," Ethan said. He sounded surprised. Anyone would have been surprise after what she had just been through and even this ghost knew that.

"I looked you up," Samantha said. "You're real. I mean, you were real. You worked here."

"I did." Ethan moved closer, but carefully, like he was afraid of spooking her. "For three years. I loved this job. I thought I was making a difference."

"What happened?" Samantha asked. "Tell me everything." Now she was beginning to become more interested, and the fear that she originally felt was beginning to fade.

Ethan sat on the edge of her desk, though he didn't actually touch it. He looked solid enough to be real, but Samantha knew if she reached out, her hand would go right through him.

"I was working on an audit," he said. "Routine stuff. But I kept finding discrepancies. Environmental impact reports that didn't match the data. Safety inspections that were supposedly completed but had no documentation. The more I dug, the worse it got."

Samantha listened, her stomach twisting. The company may not be the place she originally thought it was.

"I brought it to my supervisor," Ethan continued. "He told me to drop it. Said I was reading too much into things. But I couldn't let it go. So I kept gathering evidence. I was going to take it to the board, to the EPA, to anyone who would listen."

"And then you died," Samantha said quietly.

Ethan nodded. "The night I fell, I was supposed to meet someone. A reporter. I'd copied all my files to a flash drive, and I was going to hand it over. But I never made it out of the building."

"You think someone pushed you?"

"I don't remember," he said, frustration clear in his voice. "Everything goes blank after I stepped into the stairwell. The next thing I knew, I was standing over my own body, watching paramedics try to revive me." He looked down at his hands. "I've been stuck here ever since. Trapped. Unable to move on."

Samantha swallowed hard. "Why me? Why now?"

"Because you're the first person who can see me," Ethan said. "And because you actually care. I've watched dozens of people come through this office. Most of them just want a paycheck. But you? You really believe in this work."

"That doesn't mean I can take on the entire company," Samantha said. The weight of what he was implying was beginning to get to her.

"I know it's scary," Ethan said. "But you don't have to do it alone. I'll help you. I know where all the evidence is hidden. I know which files matter. Together, we can finish what I started." Working with a ghost on a project like this seemed to be insanity.

Samantha looked at him—this ghost, this stranger who was asking her to risk everything. And somehow, looking into his eyes, she believed him.

"Okay," she said. "Show me."

Ethan's face lit up with hope. "Really?"

"Really," Samantha said. "But if we're doing this, I need to know everything. No secrets."

"Deal," Ethan said.

And for the first time since his death, Ethan Reeves smiled like he meant it. But Samantha couldn't have known that. Only Ethan did.

Chapter 5: Uncovering the Truth

The basement archives smelled like dust and old paper. Samantha sneezed twice as she followed Ethan's directions down the narrow aisles between filing cabinets.

"Third cabinet from the left," Ethan said, floating beside her. "Bottom drawer."

Samantha pulled the drawer open. Inside were boxes of old reports, organized by year. She pulled out the one labeled 2019 and started flipping through files.

"Look for the Riverside Project," Ethan said.

She found it twenty files deep. A thick folder full of documents about a water treatment facility GreenTech had built three years ago. As Samantha read, her stomach started to hurt.

The environmental impact study claimed the facility would have minimal effect on local water quality. But buried in the appendix was a completely different report—one that showed significant contamination risks. Someone had approved the project anyway.

"Derek's signature," Samantha said, pointing to the approval stamp.

"He knew," Ethan said quietly. "They all knew. But the contract was worth millions. They weren't going to let a little thing like environmental safety get in the way."

Samantha kept reading. There were complaints from local residents about contaminated drinking water. Letters from the town council asking GreenTech to investigate. All of them ignored or dismissed.

"How many projects are like this?" she asked.

"At least a dozen," Ethan said. "Maybe more. I only had time to document a few before—" He stopped himself. "Before everything ended."

Samantha took out her phone and started taking pictures of the documents. Evidence. She needed solid, undeniable evidence.

Over the next hour, Ethan guided her through the archives. Each file he showed her was worse than the last. Falsified safety reports. Buried complaints. Internal emails where executives joked about cutting corners.

"This is criminal," Samantha said, her voice shaking. "They're poisoning communities. Destroying ecosystems. And for what? Money?"

"That's exactly what I said," Ethan replied. "And look where it got me."

Samantha looked up at him. In the dim light of the basement, he seemed almost solid. Almost real. "Are you scared?" she asked.

"Of what?"

"Of me getting hurt. The same way you did." It was a normal question to ask but asking a ghost seemed a bit odd.

Ethan's expression turned serious. "Terrified. If I could call this off right now, I would. But you're the only person who can do this. And I think—" He hesitated. "I think you're braver than I was."

"I'm not brave," Samantha said. "I'm shaking."

"Bravery isn't the absence of fear," Ethan said. "It's doing the right thing even when you're scared out of your mind."

Samantha smiled despite herself. "Is that from a fortune cookie?" Okay, it was time for a joke and she needed a bit of levity because this stuff was so serious.

Ethan laughed, and the sound was warm and genuine. "Okay, maybe it's a little corny. But it's true."

They worked in comfortable silence for a while, and Samantha found herself relaxing around him. He made jokes about office politics. He pointed out which executives were the worst. He even told her about the time he'd accidentally sent an email complaining about Derek to Derek himself.

"What did you do?" Samantha asked, laughing.

"Panic. Then blame it on a computer virus." Ethan grinned. "He believed me, somehow. Or at least pretended to."

It was strange, Samantha thought. Spending time with a ghost should have been terrifying. But instead, she felt comfortable. Safe, even.

As they climbed the stairs back to the main floor, Samantha's phone buzzed. A text from Lisa. "Coffee tomorrow?"

Samantha hesitated. She wanted to tell someone about what she'd found. But who would believe her?

"You can't tell anyone," Ethan said, reading her expression. "Not yet. If word gets out that you're investigating, they'll shut you down before you can do anything."

"I know," Samantha said. But the weight of it pressed down on her. She was carrying dangerous secrets now. Secrets that had gotten Ethan killed.

Back in her office, she copied all the photos to her personal laptop and encrypted the files. Then she cleared her phone, just in case. She knew the IT people could get everything from her phone if anyone got it and she had to be sure that everything was erased. But what about the cloud?

"You're smart," Ethan said, watching her work.

"I'm paranoid," Samantha corrected. She looked at him. "What happens now?"

"Now you start asking questions," Ethan said. "Carefully. Don't let them know what you know. But start pushing for answers. Make them uncomfortable."

"And you?" Samantha asked. "What will you do?"

Ethan smiled. "I'll be right here. Watching your back." Did that mean he could protect her in some way?

The words should have sounded creepy. A ghost watching her. But instead, Samantha felt reassured. She wasn't alone in this.

As she gathered her things to leave, Ethan spoke again. "Samantha?"

"Yeah?"

"Thank you. For believing me. For helping. I know this isn't what you signed up for."

Samantha looked at him—at his eyes and the sadness that lingered around the edges—and felt something shift in her chest. "It's exactly what I signed up for," she said. "Just not the way I expected."

And as she left the office that night, she realized something unexpected.

She liked Ethan Reeves. Ghost or not, he was easy to talk to. Easy to be around.

Which was dangerous in a whole different way.

Chapter 6: Falling for a Ghost

Samantha discovered the rooftop garden by accident. It was a wonderful relief and finding it was a great discovery.

She'd been looking for a quiet place to eat lunch, somewhere she could think without Lisa or anyone else asking if she was okay. The elevator had a button for the roof, and on impulse, she'd pressed it.

The doors opened to a small green space. Not much—just some planters with herbs and flowers, a couple of benches, and a view of the city skyline. But it was peaceful. Private.

And Ethan was there.

"How did you know I was here?" Samantha asked.

"I can sense you," he said, looking a little embarrassed. "In the building. It's like I'm drawn to wherever you are."

Samantha sat on one of the benches. The sun was warm on her face. "Is that a ghost thing?"

"Honestly? I have no idea." Ethan sat beside her, though he didn't quite touch the bench. "You're the first person I've been able to interact with. I'm making this up as I go."

They sat in silence for a while. It was a comfortable silence, the kind you could only have with someone you felt safe with.

"Can I ask you something?" Samantha said.

"Anything."

"What's it like? Being a ghost?"

Ethan was quiet for a moment. "Lonely," he finally said. "For five years, I've been watching people live their lives. Going to meetings. Eating lunch. Laughing with friends. And I couldn't do any of it. I couldn't talk to anyone. Couldn't touch anything. It was like being in a glass box, watching the world go by."

Samantha's throat tightened. "I'm sorry."

"Don't be." Ethan looked at her, and his smile was genuine. "You've changed everything. For the first time in five years, I feel like I exist again. Like I matter." It seemed that ghosts had feelings too and they experienced loneliness if Ethan was correct.

"You do matter," Samantha said softly.

Their eyes met, and something passed between them. Something warm and electric and terrifying.

Samantha looked away first. This was crazy. She couldn't be falling for a ghost. That was impossible. Ridiculous.

But her heart was racing anyway.

"Tell me about your life," Ethan said. "Before all this. Before you came to GreenTech."

Samantha told him. About growing up in a small town. About studying environmental science because she wanted to fix the world. About her ex-boyfriend who couldn't understand why she cared so much about recycling and clean water and saving forests.

"He said I was too intense," Samantha said with a bitter laugh. "Can you believe that? Too intense about protecting the planet."

"He was an idiot," Ethan said.

"Maybe. But he wasn't completely wrong. I do care too much. I always have. It's exhausting sometimes."

"It's not too much," Ethan said. "It's exactly right. The world needs people who care that much. People like you."

Samantha felt tears fill her eyes. No one had ever said that to her before. No one had ever made her feel like her passion was a strength instead of a flaw.

"What about you?" she asked, brushing at her eyes. "What was your life like?"

Ethan told her about his family. His parents who still lived in the house where he grew up. His sister who was a teacher. He told her about hiking on weekends. About his obsession with terrible action movies. About his dream of starting a nonprofit focused on water conservation.

"I was going to quit GreenTech," he said. "After I exposed them. I was going to use the publicity to launch my own organization. Do things the right way."

"You still can," Samantha said. "I mean, not you personally. But we can make that happen. In your name."

Ethan looked at her with such hope it made her chest ache. "You'd do that?"

"Of course." Now she was making a promise to a ghost that she would give his memory life in an organization that she would start.

As the sun started to set, painting the sky in shades of orange and pink, Samantha felt something she hadn't felt in years. Happiness. Real, uncomplicated happiness.

"Can I try something?" she asked.

"Sure."

Samantha reached out her hand, palm up. "Put your hand over mine."

Ethan looked confused but did as she asked. His translucent hand hovered above hers.

Samantha closed her eyes and concentrated. And there—she felt it. Not pressure exactly. Not touch in the traditional sense. But warmth. A gentle, tingling warmth where his hand should be.

Her eyes flew open. "Did you feel that?"

Ethan nodded, his expression awed. "I felt something. Like heat. Like connection."

They sat there, hands almost touching, warmth flowing between them. It wasn't the same as real contact. But it was enough. It was something.

"Samantha," Ethan said quietly. "I need to tell you something."

"What?"

"I'm falling for you. I know it's impossible. I know I'm dead and you're alive and we can never actually be together. But I can't help it. You're the first person in five years who's made me feel human again."

Samantha's breath caught. She should pull away. This was insane. But instead, she smiled. "I'm falling for you too," she whispered.

Ethan's face lit up. "Really?"

"Really. Even though you're dead. Even though this makes no sense. I can't help it either."

They sat on that rooftop as the sun disappeared, hands almost touching, both of them knowing this was the craziest thing either of them had ever done.

And both of them not caring one bit.

Chapter 7: Corporate Pushback

The trouble started at Monday's staff meeting. It would be now or never time.

Samantha had spent the weekend reviewing the evidence she and Ethan had gathered. She'd decided to start small—asking questions, raising concerns, gauging how people would react. Nothing too aggressive. Just enough to get the conversation started.

When Derek asked for updates, Samantha cleared her throat. "I've been reviewing some of our past projects," she said. "And I noticed some gaps in our environmental compliance documentation. I think we should conduct a full audit to make sure everything's up to standard."

The room went quiet. Derek's smile didn't reach his eyes. "That's a very thorough suggestion, Samantha. But we have regular audits. Our compliance team is excellent." The look on his face told her everything.

"I'm sure they are," Samantha said carefully. "But I found some reports that seem incomplete. The Riverside Project, for example. The environmental impact study has some concerning discrepancies."

Derek's expression hardened. "The Riverside Project was completed three years ago. It passed all required inspections."

"Did it?" Samantha pulled out a printed copy of the report. "Because the preliminary study showed significant contamination risks, but those concerns aren't addressed in the final approval." Now she was stepping over the line.

Someone coughed. Lisa was staring at her like she'd grown a second head. The signs were obvious all around the room.

Derek took the report from her and barely glanced at it. "Different interpretations of data are common in our industry. What looks like a risk to one analyst might be perfectly acceptable to another."

"But shouldn't we err on the side of caution?" Samantha pressed. "If there's even a chance we're putting communities at risk—"

"Samantha." Derek's tone was sharp now. "I appreciate your enthusiasm. But you're new here. You don't understand how these projects work yet. Perhaps you should focus on your current assignments before second-guessing decisions made by people with far more experience."

It was a dismissal. Clear and cutting. He was putting her on notice.

Samantha forced herself to nod. "Of course. I just wanted to bring it to your attention." Better to step back now and not push any more on what she had found.

The meeting moved on. But Samantha could feel eyes on her. Curious. Concerned. Suspicious.

After the meeting, Lisa cornered her in the hallway. "What was that about?"

"I was just doing my job," Samantha said.

"Your job is to support current projects, not dig up dirt on old ones." Lisa lowered her voice. "Look, I like you. But you're making enemies. Derek doesn't appreciate being questioned in front of everyone." Was Lisa really her friend or was she acting on behalf of the corporation?

"Maybe he should appreciate transparency," Samantha said.

Lisa sighed. "You're too idealistic. This is how business works. Sometimes you have to compromise."

"Not on this," Samantha said. "Not on people's health and safety."

Lisa shook her head and walked away.

That afternoon, Derek called Samantha into his office. She'd known this was coming.

"Sit down," he said, gesturing to the chair across from his desk. His tone was pleasant enough, but there was steel underneath. "Let's talk about your concerns."

"I'm just trying to make sure we're following best practices," Samantha said.

"Best practices," Derek repeated. "Samantha, I've been in this industry for twenty years. I know what best practices look like. And sometimes, they require flexibility."

"Flexibility that compromises environmental safety?" She couldn't believe she was questioning him but before she gave it a second thought the words were out of her mouth.

Derek's smile was cold. "You're young. You see things in black and white. But the real world is complicated. We have investors to answer to. Deadlines to meet. If we stopped every project because of minor concerns, we'd never get anything built."

"Water contamination isn't a minor concern," Samantha said quietly.

Derek leaned forward. "Let me be clear. I hired you because I thought you'd be an asset to this company. Don't make me regret that decision. Focus on your current work. Stop digging into past projects. And for God's sake, stop questioning me in front of my staff." The way he said it made it clear that there was an undertone of a threatening message to her.

It was a threat, no doubt about it. Barely veiled, but a threat nonetheless.

"Understood," Samantha said, standing. Her legs felt shaky.

That night, she stayed late at the office again. Ethan appeared as soon as the building emptied out.

"I heard," he said. "I was in the meeting. And Derek's office."

"He threatened me," Samantha said. Her voice shook. "Not directly. But the message was clear. Back off or lose my job."

Ethan's expression was pained. "We can stop. If you want to walk away, I understand."

"No." The word came out stronger than she felt. "I'm not backing down. He's counting on me being scared. But if I let him intimidate me, then what was the point of any of this?"

"You could get hurt," Ethan said. "Like I did."

"Then I'll be careful." Samantha looked at him, this ghost who'd become so important to her. "But I'm not giving up. You died fighting for this. I'm not going to let that be for nothing."

Ethan moved closer, and even though she couldn't feel him properly, she felt that warmth. That connection. "You're the bravest person I've ever known," he said softly.

"I'm terrified," Samantha admitted.

"I know. But you're doing it anyway. That's what makes you brave."

They stayed like that for a long time, close but not quite touching, both knowing the fight was only beginning.

Chapter 8: The Truth About Ethan's Death

Samantha found the security footage by accident. The accident was about to reveal everything she had been questioning.

She'd been searching through archived files on the company server, looking for more evidence of environmental violations. The folder was labeled "Security Archive 2020" and she'd almost skipped past it. But something made her click.

Inside were hundreds of video files from the building's security cameras. Samantha scrolled through them, her heart starting to pound. She found the date she was looking for. The night Ethan died.

Her hands shook as she clicked to open the file.

The footage was grainy and black-and-white. The timestamp read 10:47 PM. The camera showed the top of the main stairwell.

Ethan appeared first. He looked upset. Agitated. He was carrying a folder and kept glancing back over his shoulder.

Then Derek Morrison walked into frame.

Samantha's breath caught. The video had no audio, but she could see them arguing. Derek pointing. Ethan shaking his head. Derek stepping closer, his body language aggressive.

Then Derek reached out. It wasn't clear if he pushed or if Ethan stepped back on his own. But suddenly Ethan was stumbling backward, his arms windmilling, the folder flying from his hands.

And then he was gone. Out of frame. Falling.

Derek stood frozen for a moment. Then he looked around, grabbed the folder, and left. Quickly. Deliberately. Like nothing had happened.

Samantha closed the laptop, her whole body shaking. This wasn't an accident. Derek had been there. He'd confronted Ethan. And whether he'd pushed him or just scared him into falling, he'd left him to die.

"Samantha?"

She looked up. Ethan was standing in her office doorway, concern etched on his translucent face.

"I found it," she said. "The security footage. From the night you died."

Ethan went very still. "Show me."

Samantha played the video again. Watching Ethan watch his own death was one of the hardest things she'd ever done. His expression crumbled as the footage played out.

"Derek," he whispered when it finished. "It was Derek."

"He was there," Samantha said. "And he left. He didn't call for help. He just took your folder and left you."

Ethan sank down, sitting in midair like there was a chair beneath him. "I remember now. Bits and pieces. He was furious. He said I was going to ruin everything. That I didn't understand what was at stake."

"What did you say?" Samantha asked gently.

"That people's lives were at stake. That he was putting profits over safety. He grabbed my arm and I pulled back. I was at the top of the stairs, and I just—" Ethan's voice broke. "I just fell. And he watched me fall."

Samantha wanted to reach out, to comfort him. But all she could do was let that warmth flow between them.

"This footage proves it wasn't an accident," she said. "We can take it to the police. To the press. Derek will finally face consequences."

"No," Ethan said sharply. "You're not doing anything with that footage."

Samantha stared at him. "What? Why not?"

"Because Derek is dangerous. He's already killed once, whether he meant to or not. If you go public with this, he'll come after you. I can't—" Ethan's voice shook. "I can't watch you get hurt. I won't."

"So we just do nothing?" Samantha demanded. "He gets away with your death?"

"I don't care about justice for me," Ethan said. "I care about keeping you safe."

"Well, I care," Samantha said. "You didn't deserve what happened to you. And those communities don't deserve to be poisoned because GreenTech wants to save money. I'm not backing down. Not now. Not when we're this close."

They stared at each other. The first real fight they'd had. Actually, Samantha knew it wasn't a fight but a disagreement on how to proceed and keep her safe.

"Please," Ethan said. His voice was desperate. "Please don't do this. I can't lose you."

Samantha's anger softened. "You won't lose me. I'm going to be careful. But I have to do this. For you. For everyone he's hurt."

Ethan closed his eyes. "You're the most stubborn person I've ever met."

"That's why you like me," Samantha said.

"It's one of many reasons," Ethan admitted. He opened his eyes. "If you're really doing this, then promise me you'll be smart. No confronting Derek alone. No taking risks."

"I promise," Samantha said.

But they both knew promises were easy to make and hard to keep.

Chapter 9: An Unlikely Ally

The knock on the door went unnoticed by Samantha as she was intently studying the information on her computer monitor. Everything had to be carefully evaluated and she knew that she needed to remember so much of it that her attention was even more focused than normal.

Samantha had spent the previous sixty minutes studying her computer screen while she attempted to decide her upcoming actions. The security footage proved to be incriminating yet Ethan correctly pointed out that revealing it would create dangerous situations for her.

Another knock on the door sounded, and this time it was more forceful.

Samantha quickly shut her file before saying, "Come in."

Jennifer Hayes entered the room. She was the senior VP of operations at the company. Samantha met Jennifer Hayes for the first time during her first week at work. Hayes kept a professional appearance through her expensive clothing, commanding respect from everyone who encountered her.

Now she came into the room to speak with Samantha about something. She checked the hallway before she shut the door. It was apparent that this was going to be a conversation she didn't want anyone else to hear.

Samantha agreed to listen without any hesitation. But the situation made Samantha wonder if she would receive a termination notice. It wasn't usual that this woman would go to someone's office for a conversation and they usually were called down to her office. No, this was unusual.

Jennifer Hayes took a seat in the chair facing Samantha's desk. She was silent momentarily before she began to speak about Ethan Reeves. Ethan Reeves had worked under her supervision at the company. The man showed exceptional intelligence and intense dedication to his work. As she spoke there was a sad expression on her face while she spoke about Ethan Reeves. "The death of Ethan Reeves occurred as an accident, but I never believed it was true." Shocking to say the least it was totally unexpected that this woman would tell Samantha something of this nature.

Samantha asked Jennifer to explain her reasons for sharing this information with her. What was going to happen now? Was she being set up for something or was this a confidence being shared because of concerns about company ethics?

"You've been watching my activities because you've seen my file exploration and my investigation work which matches what Ethan Reeves attempted to achieve." Hayes leaned forward to speak to Samantha. :I should have supported him during his time at the company. I saw financial irregularities yet I failed to report them because I chose my career advancement over doing what was right." Again Samantha found this unbelievably candid.

"What caused you to change your mind?" Samantha asked, half thinking that she was going to get the company line on this.

"Your determination to fight alone brought back memories of Ethan to me. I understand now that I need to stop carrying this burden of guilt. I want to assist you in your mission because I have decided to stop hiding from my responsibilities." This woman intended to be a help for Samantha in exposing what the company had hidden?

Samantha slowly considered what Jennifer Hayes was proposing and wondered if her intentions as she stated them were true. If she proceeded as she said, the same danger that threatened Samantha now would also affect her.

Hayes spoke with determination when she said, "Let him try to harm me. I have access to company documents and correspondence that you don't have. The company has always kept internal documents and Board of Directors meeting records that show Derek's knowledge of environmental violations since the beginning."

Samantha asked Jennifer why she hadn't not revealed the truth earlier.

A sad smile crossed her face as she spoke. "I acted like a coward during that time. I've finished being afraid. The justice Ethan Reeves deserves will also bring justice to all victims of GreenTech's wrongdoing."

After she had finished indicating her intentions, Hayes gave a flash drive to Samantha. The drive had the all internal company communications from previous years. There were the security reports that underwent modifications according to Derek's direct orders which he sent through email messages. The company executives used their meeting notes to hide complaints from public view. And the company used its financial resources to give money to public officials. It was all there on the drive. And Samantha couldn't believe how valuable these records would be.

Samantha had been given a complete set of evidence which would destroy Derek's reputation. The evidence includes all necessary documents to prove his wrongdoing. There was no doubt about the authenticity since it had been kept by a woman in a high managerial position at the company. Undeniable evidence was in Samantha's hands now.

Hayes left after she finished her conversation, leaving Samantha somewhat stunned. Next, Samantha shared with Ethan the details about her meeting and the evidence Jennifer provided.

Ethan Reeves was concerned about Jennifer Hayes' dangerous situation. Would she have an accident now or would something else happen to her?

"I understand your point," Samantha said. "The situation has changed because we now have gained support from others. We possess the strength to succeed in this mission." Samantha looked at Ethan. "We possess the power to achieve victory in this fight." What she had just received was giving her a sense that she could help right this wrong and be valiant in this fight.

Ethan had a mix of sadness and hopefulness when he spoke. "The exposure of Derek along with company practice reforms will enable me to find peace."

The words created a moment of silence between them. Move on. Which meant leaving. Which meant Samantha would lose him.

Samantha extended her hand while Ethan placed his hand on top of hers. The familiar heat spread through their connected hands.

Samantha said that she would ensure Ethan's sacrifice brought meaningful results through their joint efforts to complete the mission. It would be something they had done together.

Chapter 10: The Confrontation

The board meeting was scheduled for two o'clock on Thursday afternoon, and Samantha had spent three days preparing. She'd organized all the evidence into a presentation that was clear, damning, and impossible to dismiss. Jennifer had helped her put it together, adding her own documentation and testimony.

Now, standing outside the conference room, Samantha felt like she might throw up. It was that queasy feeling you get when you're about to face something highly disturbing and even shattering. She didn't know what to expect and how they would proceed but she knew she had to do this.

"You've got this," Jennifer said beside her. "Just breathe."

Samantha nodded. She could feel Ethan's presence nearby, even though she couldn't see him. He'd promised to be there, watching. Supporting her.

They walked into the conference room together. The board of directors had already taken their seats around the long table. Eight people in expensive suits, all looking at Samantha with varying degrees of curiosity and irritation. The tension in the room was obvious.

Derek sat at the head of the table. His expression was pleasant, but his eyes were cold. This was not a man who liked to be crossed or who would even tolerate a question that he found unacceptable. Samantha had already been schooled on that after her first board meeting.

"Samantha, Jennifer," he said. "This is unexpected. I don't recall scheduling this meeting."

"We requested it," Jennifer said. "We have information the board needs to hear."

One of the board members, a woman in her sixties, gestured to the empty chairs. "Please. Sit. We're listening."

Samantha connected her laptop to the projector. Her hands were shaking, but she forced them steady. This was going to be a presentation they had never expected. She was sure.

"Thank you for your time," she began. "I'm here to present evidence of environmental violations and corporate misconduct that span the past five years."

Derek's smile didn't waver, but something flickered in his eyes. Behind that smile she knew something evil lurked.

Samantha clicked to the first slide. "The Riverside Project. Our environmental impact study showed significant contamination risks. Yet the project was approved without addressing these concerns." She showed them the reports, the highlighted discrepancies, the emails where Derek had ordered the concerns buried.

The board members leaned forward, frowns deepening. It seemed this was new information for them.

"There are multiple projects like this," Samantha continued. "Cases where we falsified reports. Paid bribes. Ignored safety protocols. All while claiming environmental excellence."

"This is a serious accusation," Derek said. His voice was smooth, but there was an edge to it. "Based on what? The interpretation of a junior analyst who's been here less than a month?" He was trying to discredit her as best he could.

"Based on documentation," Jennifer said, standing. "I've been with this company for fifteen years. I've watched us cut corners and compromise our values for profit. And I have the proof." She handed a folder to each board member. "Internal memos. Financial records. All showing deliberate environmental violations."

The board members started flipping through the folders. Their expressions shifted from skepticism to shock to anger. Undoubtedly, the board had members who believed in ethical standards.

"This is taken out of context," Derek said. But his voice was losing its confidence. "Every project involves trade-offs. We balance environmental concerns with practical realities—"

"You balance them by lying," Samantha interrupted. "And when someone tries to expose the truth, you silence them."

She clicked to the next slide. The security footage. The timestamp. The grainy image of Derek and Ethan at the top of the stairwell.

The room went completely silent. What were they watching? Was this an accident or an assault that could only be deemed murder ?

"What is this?" the woman board member asked.

"Security footage from the night Ethan Reeves died," Samantha said. "Footage that was supposedly lost. It shows Derek confronting Ethan minutes before his death. It shows Derek leaving without calling for help."

She played the video. Watched the board members' faces as they saw what she'd seen. The argument. The fall. Derek walking away.

When it ended, Derek was standing. His face was red. "That video doesn't prove anything. Ethan fell. It was an accident. I was in shock—"

"You left him to die," Jennifer said. "And then you covered it up."

"This is outrageous," Derek said. "I'm the CEO of this company. I've built GreenTech into what it is today—"

"You built it on lies," one of the male board members said. He was staring at Derek like he'd never seen him before. "These documents. This footage. Derek, you've exposed us to massive legal liability. Criminal liability."

"We need to conduct a full investigation," the woman said. "Immediately. Derek, you're suspended effective now. Pending review."

Derek's mouth opened and closed. "You can't do this."

"We can and we will," another board member said. "Clear out your office. And don't destroy any documents. Everything is evidence now." A security guard would accompany him to his office and ensure that he only took personal objects out with him.

Derek looked at Samantha. For a moment, pure rage crossed his face. Then he turned and walked out, slamming the door behind him.

Samantha's legs felt like jelly. She sank into her chair. They'd done it.

"Thank you," the woman board member said to her and Jennifer. "Both of you. What you've done here took tremendous courage. We'll make sure this company does right by the communities we've harmed."

As they left the conference room, Jennifer put a hand on Samantha's shoulder. "You did it," she said. "Ethan would be proud."

Samantha nodded, but she couldn't speak. Because she knew what this meant.

Justice for Ethan. Change for GreenTech. And goodbye.

Chapter 11: Letting Go

Samantha went to the rooftop garden as the sun was setting. This would be where she would meet Ethan and they could talk openly and alone.

She knew Ethan would be there. She could feel him, that familiar warmth that had become so important to her.

He was standing near the edge, looking out at the city. When she approached, he turned. His translucent form was even more faded than usual. She could barely make out his features.

"It's happening," he said softly. "I can feel it. I'm being pulled somewhere."

Samantha's throat tightened. "Already?"

"We did it," Ethan said. "Derek is gone. The board is committed to fixing everything. Justice is finally being served." He smiled, but it was sad. "I can finally move on."

"I don't want you to go," Samantha whispered.

"I don't want to leave you," Ethan said. "But I have to. This is what I've been waiting for. Peace." The two of them had known for some time now that this would be the way it would end.

Samantha sat on the bench, and Ethan sat beside her. They were quiet for a while, just being together one last time.

"Thank you," Ethan finally said. "For everything. For believing in me. For fighting when I couldn't. For giving me these last few weeks of feeling alive again."

"You gave me something too," Samantha said. "You made me braver. You showed me what real courage looks like."

"Promise me something," Ethan said.

"Anything."

"Don't close yourself off. Don't let this make you afraid of love. Find someone who sees how amazing you are. Someone you can touch and hold and build a life with." He was giving her permission to love again and this time someone who was really there.

Tears slid down Samantha's cheeks. "I'll never forget you."

"Good," Ethan said. "Because I'll never forget you either. Even where I'm going. Whatever comes next. You'll always be part of me."

Samantha reached out her hand, and Ethan placed his over it one last time. That warmth spread between them, stronger than ever. Like he was trying to pour everything he felt into this final connection.

"I love you," Samantha said. "I know that's crazy. But I do."

"It's not crazy," Ethan said. "I love you too. More than I ever thought possible. You brought me back to life, Samantha. Even if it was only for a little while."

The sun was sinking below the horizon, painting the sky in striking shades she'd never seen before. Somehow different but the same colors as the first time they'd come up here together.

"It's time," Ethan said. "I can feel it calling me."

"I'm not ready," Samantha said. But she knew it didn't matter. This was happening whether she was ready or not.

"You're going to be okay," Ethan said. "You're strong. You're brave. And you're going to do amazing things."

"Go," Samantha said, even though every fiber of her being wanted to beg him to stay. "Find your peace. You've earned it."

Ethan smiled. A real smile, full of warmth and love and gratitude. "Goodbye, Samantha Andrews. Thank you for everything."

"Goodbye, Ethan Reeves," Samantha whispered.

The light started to build around him. Soft at first, then brighter and brighter until he was glowing like the sun. Samantha couldn't look away. She wanted to remember every detail. The way he smiled. The kindness in his eyes. The love he'd given her.

And then, in a burst of golden light, he was gone.

Samantha sat alone on the rooftop, tears streaming down her face. But mixed with the grief was something else. Peace. Relief. Joy, even. Because Ethan was finally free. Finally at rest.

The sun disappeared below the horizon. Samantha stayed there in the growing darkness.

She'd loved a ghost. And he'd changed her life forever.

That was enough.

Chapter 12: New Beginning

Three months had passed since that sunrise morning when Ethan finally found peace. Three months of healing, growing, and learning to carry forward the love they'd shared without letting grief hold her back.

Samantha stood in her newly expanded office—still on the tenth floor, but twice the size now. As Director of Environmental Compliance, she'd earned this space. The plaques on her wall told the story: Recognition from the Environmental Protection Agency. An award from the State Green Business Council. A framed letter from a community that had been affected by one of GreenTech's old projects, thanking her for making things right.

But her favorite thing in the office was simpler. On her desk sat a small potted fern, healthy and green. She'd named it Ethan. It made her smile every morning.

A knock at her door pulled her from her thoughts. Jennifer Hayes poked her head in, smiling. "Got a minute?"

"Always," Samantha said, gesturing to the chair across from her desk.

Jennifer had become more than a colleague over these past months. She'd become a friend, a mentor, and sometimes the voice of wisdom Samantha needed. The guilt Jennifer had carried for years had transformed into purpose. Together, they'd rebuilt GreenTech from the inside out.

"I wanted you to see these before the board meeting," Jennifer said, sliding a folder across the desk. "Our Q3 environmental impact reports. Every single project is in full compliance. No shortcuts, no buried reports, no compromises."

Samantha opened the folder, her practiced eye scanning the data. It was true. Everything was clean, transparent, accountable. This was what Ethan had died fighting for. This was what they'd accomplished together.

"He'd be proud, you know," Jennifer said quietly. "Ethan. He'd be so proud of what you've done here."

Samantha's throat tightened, but she smiled through it. "We did it together. All of us."

"You led the way," Jennifer countered. "You were brave enough to fight when it mattered. That takes courage I'm not sure I would've had on my own."

After Jennifer left, Samantha finished up her afternoon work and decided to take a walk. The building felt different now. Lighter. Where there had once been cold corporate sterility, there was warmth. People smiled in the hallways. Teams collaborated openly. The fear that had hung over everything under Derek's leadership had lifted.

Derek himself was gone, facing multiple lawsuits and regulatory investigations. Samantha didn't take pleasure in his downfall, but she didn't lose sleep over it either. Justice wasn't always pretty, but it was necessary.

She found herself walking toward the stairwell, then thought better of it. The elevator would do fine today. Some places still held too many memories.

Instead, she headed for the rooftop garden.

The garden had become her sanctuary. She'd had it expanded and properly maintained, turning it into a real green space where employees could take breaks, have lunch, or just breathe. Right now, in the late afternoon light, it was peaceful and golden.

Samantha sat on one of the benches, closing her eyes and letting the sun warm her face. She could feel Ethan here sometimes. Not as a ghost—she knew he'd moved on—but as a presence. A warmth. A memory that comforted rather than haunted.

"I miss you," she whispered to the air. "But I'm okay. I'm doing what we started. I'm living the life you wanted for me."

A warm breeze touched her face, gentle as a caress. Samantha smiled.

"Samantha?"

She opened her eyes. A man stood at the garden entrance, looking a bit uncertain. He was maybe thirty-five, with dark hair and blue-grey eyes. She'd seen him around the building but didn't know his name.

"I'm sorry to interrupt," he said. "I'm David Marshall. I just started in the environmental consulting division last week. I've been hoping to meet you—you're kind of a legend around here."

Samantha laughed, standing up and extending her hand. "I don't know about legend. Just someone who cares about getting things right."

"That's exactly what I mean," David said, shaking her hand. His grip was warm and firm. "I've been reading through the policy changes you implemented. It's impressive. It's the reason I wanted to work here, actually. GreenTech used to have a pretty bad reputation in environmental circles, but now? It's become a model."

"That means a lot," Samantha said, and she meant it. "It was a team effort."

"I was hoping you might have time for coffee sometime," David said, a little nervously. "I have about a thousand questions about best practices, and I'd love to learn from you."

Samantha felt a flutter in her chest—something she hadn't felt in months. Not the earth-shaking connection she'd had with Ethan, but something gentler. The possibility of friendship. Maybe, someday, something more.

"I'd like that," she said. "How about tomorrow morning? There's a coffee shop on the corner that's pretty good."

"Perfect," David said, his face lighting up. "Thank you. I'll see you tomorrow."

He left, and Samantha sat back down on the bench, processing what had just happened. Her heart was racing a little. She wasn't ready to fall in love again—not yet. But she was ready to be open to the possibility. Ready to meet someone new and see where it might lead.

"Is this okay?" she asked the air, the garden, the memory of Ethan that lived in her heart. "Am I allowed to move forward?"

Another warm breeze answered her, stronger this time. It rustled through the plants and wrapped around her shoulders like an embrace. And somehow, Samantha knew. Ethan would want this for her. He'd told her as much in those final moments.

Find happiness, he'd said. Fall in love with someone you can touch. Build a life.

She wasn't forgetting him. She never would. But she was learning to carry that love forward rather than letting it hold her back. It was what he'd wanted. It was what she wanted too.

Lisa appeared in the garden entrance, waving. "Hey! A few of us are going out for drinks to celebrate the Q3 reports. Want to come?"

Lisa had apologized months ago for not supporting her during the crisis with Derek. She'd cried, actually, telling Samantha how ashamed she'd been of her own cowardice. Their friendship had deepened since then, built on honesty and mutual respect.

"I'd love to," Samantha said, standing up. "Let me grab my bag."

As she walked toward the door, she paused and looked back at the garden one more time. The sun was setting now, painting everything in shades of gold and rose. It was beautiful. It was peaceful. It was alive.

Just like her.

That evening, surrounded by colleagues who had become friends, Samantha felt something she hadn't felt in a long time: contentment. Not the desperate, intense passion she'd shared with Ethan—that had been its own unique gift. This was different. Quieter. Sustainable.

She thought about David and their coffee date tomorrow. She thought about the work still ahead at GreenTech. She thought about the environmental projects she wanted to launch next quarter. She thought about the life she was building, brick by brick, choice by choice.

Later that night, as she unlocked her apartment door, her phone buzzed with a text from Rachel, the security guard who'd become an unexpected friend.

"The garden was looking beautiful this afternoon. Felt peaceful up there. Hope you're doing well, honey."

Samantha smiled and typed back: "I'm doing really well. Better than I've been in a long time. Thank you for everything, Rachel."

Rachel had been there through it all. She'd believed Samantha when no one else would. She'd offered wisdom about love and loss that had helped Samantha through the darkest moments after Ethan left. Some angels, Samantha had learned, wore security uniforms and carried walkie-talkies.

As Samantha changed into comfortable clothes and settled onto her couch with a cup of tea, she realized something profound. She'd spent so much of her life before GreenTech feeling like she wasn't enough. Not successful enough, not making enough of a difference, not lovable enough.

Ethan had changed all that. He'd seen her, really seen her, and loved what he found. He'd believed in her courage when she didn't believe in it herself. He'd shown her that she was capable of extraordinary things.

And even though he was gone, that gift remained. She carried his faith in her like a light inside her chest. It illuminated every decision, every challenge, every new beginning.

Her phone buzzed again. This time it was Jennifer: "Proud of you, kiddo. Get some rest. Big week ahead."

Samantha set down her tea and walked to her bedroom window. The city sparkled below, millions of lights in the darkness. Somewhere out there, people were falling in love. Somewhere out there, people were fighting for what they believed in. Somewhere out there, people were healing and growing and becoming who they were meant to be.

She was one of them now. Not perfect. Not fearless. But brave enough to keep showing up. Brave enough to stand up for what mattered. Brave enough to love again when the time was right.

As she climbed into bed, Samantha whispered one last goodnight to Ethan. Not to his ghost—he was beyond that now—but to his memory. To the love they'd shared. To everything he'd taught her about courage and purpose and the power of connection.

"Thank you," she said softly. "For everything. For seeing me. For believing in me. For loving me. I'll carry you with me always. Not as grief, but as gratitude. Not as loss, but as love."

In the darkness of her room, she felt that familiar warmth one more time. A gentle presence that wrapped around her heart like a promise: You're going to be okay. You're going to be more than okay. You're going to be extraordinary.

And then it faded, not in sadness, but in peace.

Samantha fell asleep with a smile on her face, dreaming of tomorrow's coffee date, next quarter's projects, and all the possibilities that lay ahead. She'd learned the most important lesson of all: Love doesn't end when someone leaves. It transforms. It grows. It becomes part of who you are and how you move through the world.

Ethan had loved her across the boundaries of life and death. That love had made her braver, stronger, more certain of her worth. And now she would carry that gift forward, sharing it with others, letting it guide her toward whatever came next.

Some connections, she'd learned, really do transcend all boundaries.

And some loves change you forever—not by staying, but by teaching you who you're capable of becoming.

In her dreams that night, Samantha walked through the rooftop garden at sunrise. The flowers were in full bloom, and the air smelled like possibility. Someone was waiting for her on the bench—not Ethan, but someone new. Someone real. Someone she could touch and hold and build a future with.

But before she walked toward that new beginning, she looked up at the sky and whispered one final thank you to the man who had shown her that love, in all its forms, was always worth the risk.

And somewhere, in a place beyond words, Ethan smiled.

About the Author

P. A. Farrell is an accomplished flash fiction author whose compelling micro-narratives have captivated readers across the literary landscape. With over forty publications in prestigious online journals and literary magazines, Farrell has established herself as a master of the abbreviated form, crafting complete worlds and complex emotions within the constraints of brief word counts.

Her expertise in flash fiction extends beyond individual pieces to comprehensive collections, where she shows remarkable range and consistency in delivering powerful, bite-sized stories that linger long after the last sentence. Each collection showcases her ability to explore diverse themes, characters, and settings while maintaining the precision and impact that define exceptional flash fiction.

Farrell's work resonates with readers who appreciate literature that delivers maximum emotional and intellectual impact in minimal space. Her stories often examine the pivotal moments that define the human experience, capturing the essence of larger truths through carefully chosen details and expertly crafted prose. The breadth of her publication history speaks both to her prolific output and the consistent quality that editors and readers expect from her work.

Through her continued contributions to the flash fiction genre, P.A. Farrell has become a trusted voice for readers seeking literature that respects their time while enriching their understanding of the human condition. Her collections offer the perfect opportunity to experience the full range of her storytelling abilities in a single, cohesive volume.

In her other life, P. A. Farrell is a clinical psychologist who has written several self-help books and continues to contribute to media outlets such as Medium.com and Butterfly, where she posts articles on all aspects of healthcare, mental health, and a variety of other topics. Her Author's Page is here: https://tinyurl.com/4ewdunb8

Books by P. A. Farrell

Snowbound Hearts
   The Secrets We Keep
   The Secrets We Keep 2
   Whispers Across the Sea
   Love by the Latte
   Love Me Once Again
   Echoes of Expectation—Waiting
   Unexpected Short Tales of Surprise

A Special Request

I f this book has touched your heart, sparked your curiosity, or simply entertained you along the way, I'd be incredibly grateful if you could take a moment to share your thoughts with a review on Amazon or wherever you discovered this book. Your words not only help other readers find books they'll love, but they also mean the world to authors like me who pour their hearts into every page. Thank you for being part of this journey, and for helping stories find their way to the readers who need them most. Her Author Page on Amazon: https://tinyurl.com/4ewdunb8